Pets RULE!

Kittens Are Monsters!

Read all the  Pets RULE! books

1

Pets RULE!
My Kingdom of Darkness

Written by Susan Tan
Illustrated by Wendy Tan Shiau Wei

SCHOLASTIC

2

Pets RULE!
The Poodle of Doom

Written by Susan Tan
Illustrated by Wendy Tan Shiau Wei

SCHOLASTIC

3

Pets RULE!
Kittens Are Monsters!

Written by Susan Tan
Illustrated by Wendy Tan Shiau Wei

SCHOLASTIC

4

Pets RULE!
The Rise of The Goldfish

Written by Susan Tan
Illustrated by Wendy Tan Shiau Wei

SCHOLASTIC

Kittens Are Monsters!

Written by
Susan Tan

Illustrated by
Wendy Tan Shiau Wei

BRANCHES
SCHOLASTIC INC.

To Socks, Pippin, Pekkala, Mouse, Merlin,
Morty, Lyra, and all their Incredible Humans – ST

To my pup, Lucky, whose smiling is like sugar.
It makes our life full of sweetness. – WTSW

Text copyright © 2023 by Susan Tan
Illustrations copyright © 2023 by Wendy Tan Shiau Wei

Library of Congress Cataloging-in-Publication Data

Names: Tan, Susan, author. | Wei, Wendy Tan Shiau, illustrator.
Title: Kittens are monsters! / by Susan Tan; illustrated by Wendy Tan Shiau Wei.
Description: First edition. | New York: Branches/Scholastic Inc., 2023. | Series: Pets rule! ; 3 | Audience: Ages 5-7. | Audience: Grades 2-3. | Summary: Despite being warned that kittens are monsters, Ember the Chihuahua (who still aims for world domination) agrees to babysit a family of kittens for three days after the mother cat offers him an army in return.
Identifiers: LCCN 2022011853 | ISBN 9781338756395 (paperback) | ISBN 9781338756401 (library binding)
Subjects: LCSH: Chihuahua (Dog breed)—Juvenile fiction. | Dogs—Juvenile fiction. | Kittens—Juvenile fiction. | Cats—Juvenile fiction. | Babysitting—Juvenile fiction. | Humorous stories. | CYAC: Chihuahua (Dog breed—Fiction. | Dogs—Fiction. | Cats—Fiction. | Babysitters—Fiction. | Humorous stories. | LCGFT: Animal fiction. | Humorous fiction.
Classification: LCC PZ7.1.T37 Ki 2023 | DDC [Fic]—dc23
LC record available at https://lccn.loc.gov/2022011853

ISBN 978-1-338-75640-1 (hardcover) / ISBN 978-1-338-75639-5 (paperback)

10 9 8 7 6 5 4 3 2 1   23 24 25 26 27

Printed in China   62
First edition, April 2023
Edited by Rachel Matson
Cover design by Maria Mercado
Book design by Jaime Lucero

Table of Contents

CHAPTER 1

Destiny Pounces!

t was the middle of the night. On a normal night, I'd be asleep, curled up on Lucy's pillow. But this was not a normal night. It was a night of DESTINY.

Outside the bedroom window was an orange cat. She had large, glowing eyes.

"I have a task for you," she whispered through the window. Her voice was low and mysterious. "If you prove yourself worthy, I will give you your own army."

"An army?" I gasped.

"Yes," she whispered.

This was it! My tail wagged in excitement. I am a future Dark Lord and I am destined to rule the world. But world domination is hard by yourself. With an army, I knew that the world would be mine in no time.

"Yes!" I said. "I'll do the task."

"Good," the cat said with a happy purr. "The task is this: tomorrow, I will leave my kittens with you. You must watch over them. I will return on Saturday."

My tail froze. This was not what I had expected.

"You want me to *babysit*?" I asked.

"Not just babysit," the mysterious cat said. "Train them. Teach them all you know. If you do, the world will be yours."

My tail started wagging again. "I WILL!" I said. I could do this!

"Good," she said. "I'll be watching."

Then, in a flash of orange fur, she was gone.

I went back to the bed and curled up next to Lucy. My heart was racing.

When I finally fell asleep, I dreamed of greatness.

The next morning, I leapt out of bed. I couldn't wait to tell the other pets about the mysterious cat!

But first, I had my morning routine with Lucy.

We took our walk. Then I kept Lucy company while she fed Bubbles the goldfish, the newest Chin pet. Mr. Chin had brought her home just the night before. She lived in a small tank in Mr. Chin's office.

"Good morning, Bubbles!" I barked as Lucy sprinkled fish food.

"Blub, blub," Bubbles said. She doesn't talk much.

I followed Lucy downstairs for breakfast and sat by her chair. Sometimes she even feeds me cheese when her parents aren't looking.

The Chins sat down to eat. It felt like a normal morning.

Little did I know, it would soon become CHAOS.

CHAPTER 2

Birthday Bash

So, Lucy," Mrs. Chin said with a smile. "Are you excited for your birthday party on Saturday? I can't believe you're turning eight!"

"Your birthday is in three days?!" I gasped. In all my excitement about the kittens, I'd forgotten!

7

I'd only just learned about birthdays. Before I came to live with the Chins, I was in a shelter. No one there knew when I was born. So I don't have a birthday.

But that's okay, because when I rule the world, *every* day will be my birthday. And Lucy's, of course.

I HAD to get Lucy the perfect present. But what?

"I'm excited," Lucy said. "But I'm a little nervous for my party. I've never had my whole class over before. And Lia, the new girl, is coming, and I really want to be friends. I don't know . . . Do you think people will think it's silly if I go with the volcano theme? Should I do something more normal?"

"No, your volcano party theme sounds wonderful," Mrs. Chin said.

"Yeah, do what makes you happy," Kevin said.

"Well, Arjun's coming over tomorrow to plan," Lucy said. "I'm sure we'll figure it out." She looked like she still wasn't sure about the whole thing. But then she got excited again.

"Have you thought about getting the volcano kit for my birthday present?" She looked at her parents hopefully. "It's the BEST model volcano, and I promise I won't make a mess."

"We'll think about it," her dad said. The way he said it did not sound like "yes."

"Oh, okay," Lucy said. She tried not to look disappointed, but I knew she was.

Maybe I could help convince Mr. Chin.

"GET LUCY THE VOLCANO SET OR FACE MY WRATH!" I barked.

"Aw, Ember is excited for your birthday, too!" Mr. Chin said, patting my head.

I sighed.

These humans are not always the brightest—except for Lucy, of course.

After breakfast, the humans all left for the day.

Finally, I could tell everyone about the mysterious cat! I ran upstairs to find Neo the canary, BeBe the beetle, and Smelly Steve, Kevin's hamster.

"Everyone, I have HUGE news! Something has happened!" I said. "Actually, *two* huge things —destiny and Lucy's birthday."

"Oooh," Steve said. "I can't wait to hear about—"

Suddenly, we heard a loud bloodcurdling SCREAM!

CHAPTER 3

A Special Delivery

We ran outside to find whoever had screamed.

I looked around for an attack!

But the sound was just Zar, the Russian wolfhound. He was cowering by the porch.

"Zar, are you okay?!" Smelly Steve asked.

"Over there!" Zar squeaked. "I came by to say hi, and then I saw *that*." He pointed to a cardboard box in the middle of the yard.

"Don't go over there!" Zar said. "There's a monster inside! With too many heads!"

"A monster?" Neo gasped.

"Wait," I said. I bounded over to the box. "It's not a monster, Zar. It's . . ."

I peered inside. Small, furry faces stared back at me.

"KITTENS!" I declared.

"What?!" Steve said. "The Chins are getting more pets? That's amazing!"

"No, Steve, they're our task!" I said. I finally told them about the mysterious cat.

"Your own army?" BeBe said. "Wow!"

"We can help you babysit," Steve said.

"As long as you are sure they're not monsters," Zar said. Zar is scared of lots of things, like spiders and mice.

"I promise," I said. "They're not monsters."

Just then, Izzy, Arjun's dog, bounded into the yard.

"Hi, everyone!" she called. "I heard noise! Is there a party?"

"I got scared by monsters," Zar said. "But it was a false alarm."

"Rad," Izzy said. Izzy is an Old English sheepdog, and she uses words like *rad* a lot. *Rad* means "cool!" or "great!" She also loves dancing and singing.

Neo explained what was going on. Izzy was excited to help.

We crowded around the box, looking at the kittens. They were tiny. Some had orange and white stripes. Others were brown with lighter streaks.

They looked up at us with big eyes and mewed softly.

"Awwww," Steve said.

"Wow," Zar whispered. "They are ADORABLE."

"Greetings, kittens," I said. "For the next few days, you will be in my care. I'll teach you everything I know! Just follow my rules and stay away from the humans. Understand? They can't know you're here."

The smallest kitten gave a soft *mraow!* I think that means, "Sounds great!"

"Zar, can you turn the box on its side?" I asked. "Then the kittens can crawl out."

"On the count of three!" Izzy said. "One, two . . ."

"Fools!" A high-pitched voice hissed from behind us. "Don't unleash those kittens! They will be your nightmare!"

I whirled around, and came face to face with a real, live monster.

CHAPTER 4

Cats, Cats, Everywhere!

A giant ball of white fluff sat on the fence. It had green eyes, and it looked ANGRY.

It had clearly been listening to us.

"Ogre!" BeBe gasped from where she sat on top of Neo's head.

18

"You know this creature?" I whispered.

"He's the cat who lives next door," Neo said. "He rules his house with an iron paw!"

"But Ogre is an indoor cat!" Steve said. "What's he doing outside?"

Ogre bared his teeth.

"Maybe the house is too small for me," he said.

I gasped.

"You want to rule the world, too?!" Maybe this giant fluffy cat was my NEMESIS. A nemesis is someone who also wants to rule the world. You

have to defeat your nemesis before you can become dark overlord of all things.

"I don't want to rule the world, silly dog," Ogre said. "I just want MY house and MY yard and MY neighborhood to be LEFT ALONE. And if you let those kittens out of the box, they will go all over the place!"

"Oh," I said. I was relieved, but also kind of disappointed. A worthy nemesis seemed fun to have.

"The kittens won't be here long," I said. "Besides, this is my yard, not yours."

Ogre's already scrunched-up face squished even more.

"You will fail," he said. "You'll never complete your task. I'll make sure of it!"

He leapt down from the fence, back to his yard.

I didn't know what to say. Ogre may not be my nemesis, but he was NOT very nice.

"Don't worry, friends," I said, turning back to the other pets. "We'll show him! We'll take such good care of the kittens that—"

"Wait," Izzy said, looking into the box. "Weren't there five of them?"

We looked inside. The smallest cat was missing.

"Where did the tiny one go?" Steve asked, looking around.

And then, from inside the Chins' house, we heard a loud *CRASH*.

CHAPTER 5

Kittens Aren't Monsters . . . Right?

We raced upstairs to Mr. Chin's office.

The smallest kitten had knocked over a lamp and was trying to climb up to reach—

"Bubbles!" I yelled.

The kitten scratched at the tank. Luckily, she couldn't reach inside.

"Bad kitten!" Neo yelled. She tugged the kitten's ear. Izzy pulled the kitten down with her paw.

"Sorry, Bubbles," Neo said.

"Blub, blub," Bubbles said.

"That was close. How did she get in the house?" I asked.

"It was Ogre! He must have opened the porch door," Neo said.

"Ogre! How dare he?" I said with a gasp. "I'll show him who's—"

Just then, I heard another crash.

"Heeeeeelllppp!" Smelly Steve called.

We ran downstairs.

There were kittens EVERYWHERE.

One was on the kitchen counter, pawing through Kevin's baking supplies. One was dangling from the kitchen light.

Zar was up on one of the dining room chairs, trying to hide as a kitten leapt up and swiped at his tail with her tiny paws.

"Emergencyyyyyy!" Ste͏
by in his plastic ball. A
chasing him like he w͏

I whirled around ͏
Ogre was standing there,
with a flick of his paw, he rolle͏
shut with an evil *thump*.

"Good luck keeping them secret now.
Bwahahahaha!" Ogre called. He raced off.

n still make this work!" I shouted

chaos. "We can—aaah!"

reamed as the smallest kitten pounced

my tail.

I shook her off. We had to do something. Then, I had it!

"Izzy, sing!" I yelled.

"AWHOOOOOOOOOOOO!!" Izzy sang.

Izzy's voice was like nails on a chalkboard. I covered my ears and hoped the kittens would freeze in shock.

But instead, the kittens grinned.

Then, they YOWLED back.

"AAAH!" Izzy yelled.

Zar cowered even lower on the dining room chair.

"Ember!" he called out. "I think they're monsters after all!!"

CHAPTER 6

Cheese Solves (Most) Problems

I waited for the kittens' terrible yowling to end. What were we going to do?

Then, a small voice cut through the chaos.

"Ember, I have an idea!" BeBe yelled. She leapt from Neo's back onto Izzy's head.

"To the fridge, Izzy!" BeBe called. Izzy galloped through the sea of kittens.

27

In a minute, Izzy and BeBe were back with something familiar.

"Cheese?!" Steve yelled as he flew across the room. "Save some for meeee!"

"Over here, kittens!" BeBe called. "Everyone loves cheese, right?!"

The kittens came running.

I leapt to the porch door and rolled it open.

"This way!" I called.

Izzy ran into the yard, and the kittens followed. I rolled the door shut.

We'd gotten the kittens out of the house!

"Here, kittens!" BeBe called. She and Izzy gave each kitten a tiny piece of cheese. The kittens didn't eat the cheese, though. They just batted the pieces around like toys.

Steve watched sadly. "What a waste," he sighed. I agreed.

But there was no time to cry over lost cheese.

"Okay," I said. I tried to sound like I knew what I was doing. "We can do this! If we each take on one job with the kittens, we can manage them as a team."

"Yeah!" Neo chirped. "That's a great idea, Ember!"

I beamed. I'm trying to get better at teamwork, and I was glad that Neo liked my plan.

I wanted to celebrate. But then, I saw a fluffy white tail disappear over the fence.

Ogre was watching us.

I didn't know what to do. How would we manage these kittens AND Ogre for three whole days?

But I knew one thing for sure.

Suddenly, our lives had WAY too many cats.

CHAPTER 7

Super-Kitten!

We need a plan," I said. "Neo, will you watch out for Ogre? Stay high up and yell if you see him."

"On it!" Neo said. She flew away with BeBe on her back.

"I'll be in charge of the kittens' meals," Smelly Steve said.

"I'll teach the kittens to dance," Izzy said.

"I'll teach them to play patty-cake!" Zar said, raising his paw over one of the kittens.

"NO, ZAR!" we all shouted.

But it was too late.

Zar brought his giant paw down, and the kitten went flying through the air!

"I can't look!" Steve yelled.

I watched in horror as the kitten flew and then . . . landed on her feet. She was okay!

She ran back to Zar, and the other kittens followed.

They all wanted to play patty-cake.

"Okay, so Zar is in charge of games," I said. Another kitten went sailing through the air, purring happily.

"I'll teach them about world domination," I said. "In between that, I'll have time to get Lucy the perfect birthday gift."

"That's easy—sing to Lucy!" Izzy said.

"Or do flips!" Smelly Steve said. "That's what I do for Kevin whenever a baking recipe doesn't work. It makes him smile every time."

"Uh . . . we'll see," I said.

Smelly Steve flipped in his ball, and the orange kitten ran over and flipped, too.

"Amazing!" Smelly Steve said to the kitten. "I'll teach you everything I know. I'll name you Stinky!"

Stinky the kitten flipped again.

"Go, Stinky!" Smelly Steve cheered.

"Great idea, Steve," I said. "Let's give these kittens names!"

Next, it was time for their first lesson in world domination. "Okay," I said. "Pretend Steve's ball is the world. You want to take it over. What do you do?"

The kittens started chewing on Zar's tail.

Kittens, I was learning, are very stubborn.

The day flew by as we played with the kittens. All the while, Neo and BeBe looked out for Ogre. He was lurking nearby, I could feel it.

We said goodbye to the kittens before the Chins got home. Izzy carried them to her house, since Arjun and his dads were away for the night visiting family.

I went inside and waited at the front door for Lucy to get home from school, like always.

She walked in, and I licked her nose. "I'll get you the perfect gift," I said. "I promise!"

But I was too tired to think of anything.

I didn't even have the energy to threaten Mr. Chin at dinner when Lucy asked, "Dad, did you think any more about the volcano kit?"

Mr. Chin was distracted. He just said, "Huh?" as if he hadn't even been listening.

What was I going to do?

I'd only spent one day with the kittens, and I was exhausted! Plus, I still didn't have any gift ideas for Lucy!

And tomorrow, it would begin all over again.

37

CHAPTER 8

The Great Curtain Caper

The next morning, I had a new plan. We'd focus on one kitten lesson: hiding. I knew that if the humans found the kittens, they'd take them to the vet . . . or worse, the shelter! Then I would have really failed my task.

Izzy brought the kittens to the backyard. She looked EXHAUSTED. So while Izzy napped, Steve, Neo, BeBe, Zar, and I taught them a new game.

"One, two, three . . . HIDE!" I shouted.

The kittens ducked or curled up in the grass. Sidekick froze against the fence. Patty leapt up and clung to Zar's fur.

They were GREAT at hiding!

We played this game all morning. Then patty-cake. Next, the kittens climbed all over Zar and he tried to shake them off—but gently. Zar was very good with the kittens.

Finally, Steve, Neo, and BeBe took the kittens to our basement so they'd be inside before the Chins got home.

Now I was exhausted. So I went upstairs to talk to someone who I knew would listen.

"I've taught the kittens just ONE thing: hiding," I said to Bubbles. "Their mother said I need to teach them EVERYTHING I know. I don't know how I'll complete this task!"

"Blub," Bubbles said.

"Also, I still have to get Lucy the perfect gift," I went on. "But what?"

"Blub," Bubbles said.

"Well, thank you for listening, Bubbles," I said.

I left the office and stopped.

Mr. Chin was home—and he was in the hall. He was tiptoeing upstairs to . . . the attic?

I wanted to see what he was up to. But then, I heard voices from the living room. Lucy was home, too. I'd missed greeting her at the door!

I ran downstairs.

Lucy and Arjun were in the living room with a box of party supplies.

"I think we need more balloons. There's only one in here," Arjun said.

"Huh." Lucy frowned. "I thought we had more. I'll put it on the list." She wrote on a notepad with her sparkly blue pencil.

"What kind of ice cream do you want?" Arjun asked.

"Well . . ." Lucy looked unsure. "My favorites are red bean and green tea ice cream. But will people think that's weird? Should I just go with vanilla?"

"Those sound delicious!" Arjun said.

"Okay," Lucy said. But she looked worried.

Lucy put her pencil down like she didn't want to work on the party anymore.

I started forward to encourage her.

Then I froze.

Just above Lucy's head, reaching out from behind the curtains, was a PAW. Sidekick, Patty, and Thunder Road were crawling up the curtains!

I had to keep Lucy and Arjun from turning around.

But then, something else appeared behind Lucy and Arjun.

Outside the window, I saw green eyes and an evil smile.

Ogre grinned at me.

He lifted a paw and BANGED on the window.

I watched in horror as Lucy and Arjun started to turn toward the curtains.

CHAPTER 9

Of Kittens and Chaos

But just as Lucy and Arjun turned toward the window, Neo swooped in!

She flew in circles, keeping them from noticing the kittens.

"Ember! Ogre let the kittens out!" Neo called. "They're all over the house!"

Lucy and Arjun were distracted, but they wouldn't be for long.

"HIDE!" I barked at the kittens.

Amazingly, they DID.

Sidekick froze. Her orange fur blended in with the orange curtains.

Thunder Road dropped down behind the couch.

Patty climbed to the other side of the curtains so that only her claws could be seen.

We had outsmarted Ogre.

For now.

Lucy and Arjun took Neo back upstairs to her perch.

I rounded up the kittens and rushed them back to the basement.

"Bad kittens!" I said. "Remember, you have to stay hidden!"

The kittens looked at me with innocent eyes.

I sighed. This was a DISASTER. And I hadn't even said hi to Lucy!

Smelly Steve took over kitten-sitting, and I went back upstairs. I was ready to help Lucy with her party planning and to show her how much I care.

But wait. I sniffed around the living room. Where was Lucy's sparkly pencil?

It wasn't where she'd left it on the floor.

I looked under the couch, but it wasn't there, either.

Strange.

Something wasn't right.

I walked through the house, looking around.

"Where are my cookie cutters?" Kevin asked from the kitchen.

"I haven't seen them," Mrs. Chin said. "And I also can't find my glasses case. Weird!"

"Have you seen my blue pocket squares?" Mr. Chin called down the stairs.

All over the house, things were missing.

Like the party balloons . . .

My tail stood on end.

Could the kittens be to blame for the missing objects?

I hadn't taught them good lessons like ambition and world domination.

Instead, I'd taught them to be sneaky, to hide.

What if . . . I'd turned the kittens into CRIMINAL MASTERMINDS?!

A Warning

That night, it was my turn to watch the kittens.

"You're not coming up, Ember?" Lucy looked at me, puzzled. I always go upstairs with her. I keep her company while she's brushing her teeth and then curl up on her pillow. But I couldn't, not tonight. Lucy looked sad, and my ears drooped.

After a minute, she went upstairs.

I watched her go, also feeling sad. How could I explain that I had to do this?

In the basement, the kittens were finally getting sleepy. I nudged them all up onto the basement couch. Then I hopped up, too.

"We have time for one last lesson before bed. Let me tell you about ruling the world," I said. "You have to be responsible. You have to set a good example. Remember, if you rule the world, it's your job to look out for other animals, and even humans."

I looked down to see if they understood.

But they weren't listening. They were soon fast asleep.

They were so peaceful. It was hard to believe they could be so evil when they were awake.

I sniffed around the basement. There was no sign of Lucy's sparkly pencil, or any of the other things the Chins were missing.

I crept upstairs to get a drink of water before going to sleep. I was tiptoeing through the kitchen, when suddenly—

SCRIIITCH.

I turned to the window. It was the big orange cat!

"How are my kittens?" she asked. "Are you teaching them well?

"Uh, yes!" I said. "Of course. Everything is PERFECT. Why wouldn't it be?"

51

"I've heard rumors," she said. "Are my kittens learning bad habits from you?"

"No, everything's fine!" I said. "I promise!"

"Remember," she said. "You'll only get your own army if you train my kittens well."

Then, she was gone.

I sat down, stunned. Who could have told her things weren't going well?

Then, through the window, a white shape
leapt into view.

OGRE.

He had told
the mother cat
that I was failing
my task.

I knew then
and there that
SOMETHING
had to be done.

Ogre was not
my nemesis, but
he was definitely
a villain. He was
playing games with us. The kittens only
wanted to play games, too . . .

I stopped short.

That was it!

I knew what we had to do!

CHAPTER 11

Cat in the Act

The humans were out all the next day. In the morning, I gathered the pets in the backyard. The kittens played nearby with Zar.

"The kittens are up to something. I think they've been stealing things around the house. We need to catch them in the act," I whispered. "We'll use a game to set a trap."

"But how?" Steve asked.

"Will it be dangerous?" Neo asked.

"Should we challenge them to a dance-off?" Izzy asked.

"No," I said. "We'll do something even better."

We set our plan in motion.

Izzy and BeBe were in charge of bait.

"Can't I have just one taste?" Steve asked. He looked at the block of cheese on the dining room table.

"No, Smelly Steve," I said. "Be strong. Now, *places*!"

Neo flew up and hid above the kitchen cabinets.

Outside, Izzy and Zar were pretending to watch the kittens. But they weren't "watching" very closely.

Steve rolled open the porch door and "accidentally" forgot to close it. Then he hid under the dining room table.

I hid by the living room door and watched.

Soon, I heard raised voices outside.

"DANCE-OFF!" Izzy yelled.

"Uh, yeah, dance-off!" Zar yelled back.

We knew that if Izzy and Zar pretended to be distracted, the kittens would sneak inside.

Sure enough, after a few minutes, I saw Sidekick peer through the porch door.

I ran to hide behind the couch so the kittens wouldn't see me.

I heard a soft *creeeak*. Then I watched Sidekick tiptoe into the living room, with the giant piece of cheese in her mouth.

She gave a *meow*. Thunder Road and Ted came in, each holding something in their mouths. I recognized one of Lucy's flower barrettes and one of Kevin's socks. The kittens *had* been stealing things. We'd caught them in the act!

The kittens nudged one of the living room curtains aside. There was a small hole at the bottom of the wall that I'd never noticed before. Sidekick began pushing the cheese toward it.

"NOW!" I shouted.

Steve rolled into the living room. Neo swooped in, landing on Ted's head.

"Caught you!" she chirped.

I dashed out from behind the couch.

Izzy and Zar raced in from the yard, carrying the rest of the kittens by the scruffs of their necks.

"We found it," I called. "This is where they've been hiding things."

I turned and frowned at the kittens.

"Stealing is WRONG!" I said, walking over to the hole and lowering my head to look inside. "You're going to return everything you took, and—"

I stopped short.

From inside the hole in the wall, a row of tiny, bright eyes stared back at me.

CHAPTER 12

Cat-and-Mouse Game

Mice!" I shouted. I leapt back in surprise.

"Wait." I paused. I looked at the kittens.
Sidekick gave me a shy smile.

I peered into the mousehole again.

It was BEAUTIFUL.

There were the small pieces of cheese we'd
given the kittens. They were stacked neatly
inside Kevin's T. rex cookie cutter.

The floor was covered with rugs made of balloons.

There was Mrs. Chin's glasses case, filled with Mr. Chin's pocket square to make a bed.

Next to the bed, Lucy's sparkly pencil leaned against the wall, and another pocket square hung over it like a tent. Inside, a tiny pair of eyes looked out curiously.

It was a crib for a baby mouse!

"You . . ." I turned to Sidekick. "You've been helping the mice?"

Sidekick nodded.

The adult mice came out of their hole, and the kittens smiled wide.

I couldn't believe it.

"This is BRILLIANT," I said.

"Great job, Ted!" Neo said.

"I'm so proud of you, Stinky!" Steve said.

"Rad, dude," Izzy said. "Great teamwork." She high-fived Thunder Road.

"I'm afraid of mice, and even I'm proud!" Zar said, cuddling Patty.

"Kittens," I began, "you are—"

Then, I heard a familiar voice. A TERRIBLE voice.

"AHA!" Ogre said.

Ogre was in the house!

"At last!" he said, coming toward us.

For the first time, I realized how BIG Ogre was.

"I knew those mice were here somewhere!" Ogre hissed. "Now I'll deal with them once and for all! BWAHAHAHA!"

CHAPTER 13

Cat-astrophe!

Ogre skulked toward us like a giant, evil, fluffy pillow.

"These mice are why I stopped being an indoor cat," he hissed. "I knew they were out here somewhere. They used to live at my house, until I chased them out. I won't let them make their home here!"

Zar cowered, and Steve hid behind him. BeBe burrowed into Neo's feathers. The kittens looked scared. I was scared, too.

Ogre's sharp claws came out, and he glared at the mice.

We had to protect them! What could we do?!

I looked around frantically.

And then, Sidekick turned to me.

There was a gleam in her eye. An evil gleam. Suddenly, I understood.

We hadn't failed the kittens—they'd been learning from us all along!

I grinned back at Sidekick.

"Pets," I commanded, "do your worst!"

Together, we CHARGED.

"DANCE PARTY!" Izzy yelled. She and Thunder Road knocked into Ogre. This gave Patty and Sidekick time to shoo the mice back into their hole. They nudged the mice gently and carefully, like Zar had taught them.

Ogre ran toward the mice. But Stinky rolled like a ball and knocked into one of Ogre's paws, and Steve hit the other.

Ogre staggered for a step, then found his feet. He leapt over Steve and Stinky. He was ready to pounce!

But then—

"Zar, play patty-cake!!" BeBe shouted.

Patty leapt up, and Zar played patty-cake, gently tossing her with his paw.

Patty FLEW toward Ogre, knocking him against the wall.

"Kittens, SING!" Neo chirped. The kittens yowled.

"Aaaaah!" Ogre yelled, stumbling back and covering his ears.

"Sidekick, the curtain!" I yelled. We raced toward Ogre, each of us taking an end of the curtain in our mouths. We tied Ogre up tightly in the curtain.

Ogre was trapped.

We had saved the mice!

All of a sudden, we heard—

"A car!" Neo chirped. She flew to the window. "Mr. Chin is home early!"

"We need to get Ogre out of here!" I called. "Quickly! Outside!"

Zar grabbed Ogre, and we ran out the porch door.

"Into Ogre's yard!" Neo whispered. "So Mr. Chin can't see us!"

We raced out of sight and tumbled into
the yard next door.

I was about to breathe a sigh of relief.

But then I looked up. A strange human
was standing there, his back toward us.

"It's Leo, Ogre's human!" BeBe yelled.
"Hide!"

CHAPTER 14

Ogres Are . . . Sweet?

We dashed into the bushes. We left Ogre in the middle of the yard, struggling to get out of the curtain. Then, Sidekick helped to make sure all the kittens were hidden.

"Sweetums!" Leo called. "Sweetums! Where are you?"

He turned and saw Ogre, who was just shaking off the curtain.

"SWEETUMS!" Leo said. "What are you doing outside?!"

"HUMAN?!" Ogre gasped. "But . . . I thought you had left me!"

"Oh, Sweetums," the human said and picked him up. Ogre started purring.

"I told you, I was just away for a trip. Did you have fun with the cat-sitter?" Leo asked.

My jaw dropped.

"*Sweetums?*" I whispered to Neo.

Ogre was many things. But he was NOT a sweet cat.

Ogre sighed.

"Yes, human, I am your 'little Sweetums.' But to the rest of you, I am OGRE," he said, glaring into the bushes.

"Wow," Smelly Steve whispered. "That's kind of adorable."

"I'll leave the cat flap open," Leo said. "But stay close, okay?"

He gave Ogre a pat, then put him down and went inside.

Slowly, we crept out of the bushes.

"I'm sorry." Ogre sighed. "I tried to keep you from helping the kittens because I didn't want them around. And when I saw the mice had a happy home, I was jealous. You see, I thought my human had left me."

"I understand," I said. "If I thought Lucy had left me, I'd be so upset . . ."

I paused and thought about Lucy's party. I couldn't believe I *still* didn't have a gift. How would Lucy know how much I love her?

Sidekick nuzzled into me, purring. Then I realized: the kittens had helped the mice in their own way. They had brought the mice things they needed, to show they were there for them.

And it was the same with Lucy.

I'd been too distracted to be there for Lucy because I was so focused on getting her the perfect gift. But what Lucy really needed was *me*. She needed to know I was there for her.

And I wasn't the only one.

"I have to do something!" I said.

I raced inside and ran upstairs to the attic, where I knew I'd find Mr. Chin.

"I know what you're up to, human!" I declared. "You can't hide from me! And we're going to do this TOGETHER."

CHAPTER 15

The Best Birthday

The day of Lucy's party was sunny and warm.

We helped a lot.

I barked in encouragement while Kevin baked Lucy's chocolate lava birthday cake.

Steve did flips in his ball when the cake came out PERFECTLY.

76

Izzy danced when Arjun put on his party playlist made of Lucy's favorite songs.

I wagged my tail when Lucy put out red bean and green tea ice cream, to show her that everyone would like it.

And Neo led us all in singing "Happy Birthday."

"This is the best party ever!" Lia said. "Green tea ice cream is my new favorite!"

Lucy beamed.

Finally, it was time for gifts.

I pranced in excitement. I led the way as Mr. Chin brought Lucy and

her guests upstairs. Mr. Chin had a secret project, just like the one I'd had with the kittens. The clues had been there all along: he also had been distracted all week.

Mr. Chin swung open the attic door dramatically.

Lucy opened and closed her mouth like she couldn't find any words to say.

Mr. Chin had turned the attic into a volcano research room. There were red-and-orange twinkle lights, boxes for her rock collection, maps, and, of course, a brand-new volcano modeling kit.

And I, Ember the Mighty, had put my paw print, in orange paint, on the side of the volcano, so Lucy would know I always support her.

"How about more cake and ice cream?" Mrs. Chin asked after a few minutes. And everyone LOVED that idea.

We went back down to the yard.

But before the humans ate, Lucy stood and picked me up.

"Thank you all for coming to my party," she said. "It's been the best birthday ever! But it's not just *my* birthday today."

"It isn't?" I barked, looking up at her, puzzled.

"It's Ember's, too! Well, we don't know the exact date, so it felt right that we'd share one. Sound good, puppy?" she asked, looking at me.

I couldn't speak. But my tail spoke for me.

"Look how fast Ember's wagging his tail!" Kevin said.

"Look how happy he is!" Mr. Chin said.

"It's perfect," I said.

The kittens watched the party from under the porch, where they were having their own party with the mouse family.

And when Lucy gave me a piece of cheese to celebrate our party, I opened my mouth wide . . . and took a small bite.

Then I trotted to the porch to leave the rest for the mice.

CHAPTER 16

The World Waits

That afternoon, the orange cat returned.

The kittens crowded around, nuzzling her fur.

"How was your mission?" I asked.

"Perfect," she said. "I've found homes for all my kittens. They'll be close by, and with loving families. You have given them all the skills they need to look out for themselves and to be kind and caring to their humans."

"That IS perfect," I said.

"Yes," she purred. "Now, about your army."

My ears perked up. I'd almost forgotten! She gestured around her.

"See these kittens? When they grow up, they will be UNSTOPPABLE. *They* will be your army."

Sidekick gave me a happy, evil grin.

"With your kittens by my side, we will rule the world!" I said.

"Yay!" Smelly Steve said, rolling up beside me. "And then we'll have cheese, right?"

"All the cheese you want, my loyal subject," I said.

All the neighborhood pets, even Ogre, came to help deliver the kittens to their new homes. Ogre, it turns out, was GREAT at tying bows.

"First, I'll take *you* home," the mother cat said to Sidekick. "You have the shortest trip."

She looked at Ogre and smiled.

"Wait," Ogre stammered. "I can't take care of a kitten."

Sidekick looked up at him and purred.

"I think it might be the other way around," Neo said.

Ogre's fur puffed out happily.

He and Sidekick disappeared over the fence.

The rest of the kittens purred, then raced off with their mother.

I watched them go, feeling proud.

Now I could see Sidekick every day.

And I knew that with my army of kittens, the world would be mine in no time. How could I lose, when I had an army who was so good at sneaking, stealing, and taking care of others?

I went inside. Lucy was in Mr. Chin's office, helping him with a giant box. It was a huge new fish tank for Bubbles, to replace the one that Sidekick had scratched.

"Aw, Bubbles has a new home," Neo chirped, fluttering in.

"Yeah, nice tank!" Steve said, rolling up next to me.

We turned to go.

Suddenly, we heard a strange sound. A sound that chilled my blood.

"At last," Bubbles whispered. "A kingdom of my own. Soon, the whole world will be my tank. BWAHAHAHAHA!"

"Uh-oh," Neo said.

"Oh boy," Steve said.

"At last!" I gasped. "A worthy NEMESIS."

Susan Tan lives in Cambridge, Massachusetts. She grew up with lots of small dogs who all could rule the world. Susan is the author of the Cilla Lee-Jenkins series, and *Ghosts, Toast, and Other Hazards*. She enjoys knitting, crocheting, and petting every dog who will let her. Pets Rule! is her first early chapter book series.

Wendy Tan Shiau Wei is a Chinese-Malaysian illustrator based in Kuala Lumpur, Malaysia. Over the last few years, she has contributed to numerous animation productions and advertisements. Now, her passion for storytelling has led her down a new path: illustrating children's books. When she's not drawing, Wendy likes to spend time playing with her mixed-breed rescue dog, Lucky. The love for her dog is her inspiration to help this book come to life!

Pets RULE!

Kittens Are Monsters

Questions & Activities

Ember and his friends train the kittens. Look back at Chapter 7. What special trick did each of the pets teach the kittens?

Who is Ogre the cat? Why is he upset that the mice family has found a home?

The kittens are stealing things in the house. What objects can you spot in the artwork on pages 60–61?

Why is Lucy feeling nervous about serving her favorite ice-cream flavors at her birthday party? Describe a moment when you felt how Lucy feels.

Ember learns that Bubbles has plans to rule the world! What do you think her plans are? Write a paragraph about what you think will happen with Bubbles in the next book!